PETER
AND
THE
WHIMPER-WHINEYS

Coloring Book

by Sherrill S. Cannon

Illustrations by Kalpart

Strategic Book Publishing and Rights Co.

Strategic Book Publishing and Rights Co., LLC
USA | Singapore
www.sbpra.net

**For information about special discounts for bulk purchases,
please contact Strategic Book Publishing and Rights Co., LLC. Special
Sales, at bookorder@sbpra.net.**

ISBN: 978-1-952269-68-4

Check this book on the following online stores.
https://www.amazon.com/Peter-Whimper-Whineys-Sherrill-S-Cannon/dp/1609115171
http://sbprabooks.com/sherrillscannon/peter-and-the-whimper-whineys/
https://www.barnesandnoble.com/w/peter-and-the-whimper-whineys-sherrill-s-cannon/1021832448

In loving memory of my mother

Beth T. Stalker

who told this story to her children,
grandchildren, and great-grandchilden;
as well as to many of her
second grade students throughout her life.
She was delighted with my rhymed version of her story!

Also for:
Joshua Cakebread, Parker James, Colby Stalker,
Lindsay Alexis, Tucker Flynn,
Kelsey Beth, Mikaila Bryn, Kylie Brenna,
Cristiano Cannon, and Chloe Grey

Special thanks to KJ and her team of illustrators
whose artistry brought this story to life!
Thank you also to my daughters Kerry and
Cailin for their suggestions and support,
and to my sons K.C. and Kell
who asked me to write "Gammy's story"
to read to their children.

In a house in the forest all covered with vines
Lived a very small rabbit who did nothing but whine.
He'd whine and he'd cry from morning till night,
And nothing that anyone did would be right.

He'd cry and he'd whine, and he'd whine and he'd cry,
Till his mother said, "Peter, I want you to try
To stop all that whining and unpleasant noise.
Go take a nap, or go play with your toys;
If you can't stop that whining, I very much fear
That the old Whimper-Whineys will look for you here.
You'll go live with them in a land far away,
Where you'll join them in whining and crying all day."

But Peter was selfish and cranky and cross,
He wouldn't play games unless he was the boss;
He'd whine and he'd cry till he got his own way,
Then he'd yell at his sister who didn't want to play.

His mother was fixing his dinner one night
When she heard Peter screaming, it gave her a fright.
She rushed to the table and found Peter there,
Whining and crying, standing up on his chair.

"My sister has more soup than I in her bowl,
She took too much jelly to put on her roll;
She's got more than I do, it's really not fair,"
Whined Peter while sliding back down in his chair.

"That's it!" said his mother, "You're going to bed!
Perhaps you can think about what I have said.
You must stop this whining and crying you do,
For no one will ever want to be around you;
And standing on chairs is not safe, as you know;
Your mother knows best, and I say it is so.
You need to be happy and pleasant and bright;
So think about that," and she turned out the light.

So Peter lay back on his soft little bed,
While thoughts of his mother's words danced in his head.
He looked out his window and saw a full moon,
And wished he weren't punished and stuck in his room.

"I wish I were out there," he thought, and he sighed…
And all of a sudden he was standing outside!

He looked at the woods in the distance and thought,
"I wonder what's out there?" So though he'd been taught
To never go into the woods all alone,
Peter went hippity-hop from his home.

He went hippity-hoppity, hippity hop;
At the edge of the woods, he found a big rock.
When he stopped for a rest he felt something quite queer:
Something was tugging on his little ear!
It tugged on his left ear and then on his right,
And when Peter looked up, he saw a strange sight:

He saw an old man who was dressed all in green,
With a big tall green hat that was not very clean;
His eyes were all swollen and puffy and red,
And his gigantic nose stuck right out of his head.

Peter, though frightened, just said "Who're you?"

"I've heard all the whining and crying you do,"
Whined the strange little man with the great big red nose,
Who was dressed all in green in his strange little clothes.
"I'm a Whimper-Whiney, a Whimper-Whiney Man,
And I've come to take you to Whimper-Whineland."

But Peter thought, "No Way!" and pulled his ears free,
Hopped into the forest and under a tree.
He waited in hiding, saw no one appear,
So he wiggled his nose and he waggled his ear;
And not feeling anything holding him tight,
He hopped down the trail and into the night.

He hopped round a bend in the trail and he found
A circle of Whineymen, sitting on the ground.
They were sitting cross-legged, those strange little men,
Rocking back and forth, back and forth, over again.

"What are you doing?" Peter said with surprise,
As he saw their red noses and weepy wet eyes.
"We're crying a pond," whined a Whimper-Whineyman,
"We're whining and crying as hard as we can."
"You're crying a what?" Peter thought he'd heard wrong,
He was tired and thirsty from hopping so long.
But the Whineyman told Peter over again,
"We're crying a pond for the ducks to swim in!
We have so many tears in Whimper-Whineland,
We've made a small pond where there used to be sand."

Peter wasn't too sure what he thought about that,
But he saw a large table and chairs, so he sat;
For he hoped he could get something to drink and to eat.
The strange little men suddenly got to their feet
And rushed to the table, knocking into each other
And kicking and shoving, they pushed one another;

They grabbed all the food with their dirty small hands
And stuffed in their mouths all the food they could cram.
They were licking and smacking and spitting out seeds,
Eating fast as they could in their terrible greed.
They ate with their hands and they gobbled their food –
Those Whimper-Whineymen were impossibly rude!!

One climbed on the table, one stood on a chair;
They talked with their mouths full, they seemed not to care
That Peter was sitting with nothing to eat;
Not even some vegetables, much less some meat.

After a while someone shoved him a glass.
It seemed to be milk; Peter sipped it, and gasped,
"This milk is sour! It really does stink!
It's curdled and gross and it's not fit to drink!!"

One Whineyman whined, with a sigh and a sob,
Wiping grease from his chin with his sleeve like a slob,
"But Peter, it seems that you don't understand:
Everything's sour in Whimper-Whineland!
We cry our salt tears into everything here;
So everything's spoiled and sour, I fear."

Well Peter thought he'd had enough of this place:
These men with no manners, their food a disgrace;
Their whining and crying, the way they did shout;
He knew what his mother'd been talking about!

He got up from his chair and crept softly away;
He thought if he got home, he never would stray;
He'd never go into the woods all alone –
If only, if only he could find his way home!

So Peter went hippity-hoppity-hop,
He kept right on hopping and didn't dare stop.
He promised himself to be happy and good –
When he came to that rock at the edge of the wood,
He saw his house waiting, it was not far to go;
So he started hip-hopping, but then stubbed his toe...

And Peter woke up in his own little bed!
He had only been hopping in dreams in his head!!
His mother was calling him, saying to rise;
There was sunshine outside and the bluest of skies.
His mother said, "Peter, it's a beautiful day;
I do hope you're going to be happy today!"

Do you think he was?

CPSIA information can be obtained
at www.ICGtesting.com
Printed in the USA
BVHW021150250620
582311BV00014B/230